Bear & Katie
in
The Great Searsport Caper!

By Loni R. Burchett

Illustrated by Patricia Sweet-MacDonald

Third Print: April 2007

Written by Loni R. Burchett
Illustrated by Patricia Sweet-MacDonald
Edited by Nancy Grossman and Tracey Burchett

Published by Black Lab Publishing, LLC
P.O. Box 64
Alton, NH 03809
www.bearandkatie.com

Printed by Morgan Press, Inc., Manchester, NH

ISBN: 0-9742815-0-6

Dedicated to

My father and mother, Charles and Marcella
Rye, for being loving parents and my husband
Doug, my best friend.

And to Bear and Katie forever. Who truly
live up to the old saying; "A dog is a
man's best friend."

NOTE: Bear, always wears a red collar.
Katie, prefers a blue scarf.

Bear and Katie refer to their owners as
Dad and Mom.

Special Thanks to the following people:

Richard Haynes, free lance photographer, artist and friend. For all the countless hours he spent helping me to achieve my goals.

Nancy Grossman, artist, writer, editor and wonderful friend. For her inspiration and encouragement.

Acknowledgement:

The Lighthouse Preservation Society
11 Seaborn Drive
Dover, NH 03820

Maine's Lighthouse Museum
(Lighthouses of Maine)
104 Limerock Street
Rockland, ME 04841

Table of Contents

Introduction

I wrote the Bear and Katie stories so children could learn about the environment, our precious wild-life, geographical locations and family values, all while having fun with Bear and Katie. Through these stories, young readers will travel to exciting places and join in adventures with these two fun-loving black labs.

These two unique labs could be anyone's dog's. Become friends with Bear and Katie and tag along on their adventures everywhere our two friends travel!

Part One

The Great Searsport Caper

The coast of Maine is one of Bear's and Katie's favorite places to vacation. During the summer, they spend more weekends in Maine than anywhere else in the world. This weekend the family is going to visit Searsport, a small town on the coast of Maine. It's going to be a trip full of mystery for the two Black Labs from New Hampshire.

Bear is quiet and very intelligent. She loves going for rides and sightseeing. She jumps when she hears the sound of keys jangling. Katie on the other hand loves swimming and retrieving tennis balls. She loves snooping around just to see what she can get into. Bear loves adventure and Katie loves mischief.

It's a beautiful morning. Temperatures are already in the seventies. Bear and Katie can't wait to hit the beach. Mom and Dad have invited their niece and nephew along for the trip.

A short stop in Portland, to pick up Michael and Julia, make Bear and Katie very happy dogs. It's been a long time since they have seen them.

Michael and Julia are happy to take a seat in the truck. Katie rests her head on Julia's lap while Bear watches out the window. A few hours later they pull into the small town of Searsport.

"This was once a thriving town. I believe there was once a boat-building industry here and many sea captains made Searsport their home," Dad tells them.

"Yes, and there are a lot of antique shops, and stores to browse. Not to mention the lovely park overlooking the beautiful beach," says Mom with a smile.

"What a pretty place!" sighs Katie.

"It sure is!" replies Bear. "The smell of salt air is always a pleasure. I just love the ocean!"

"Isn't it nice to have Michael and Julia with us this time?" asks Katie as she turns to glance up at the two children.

Before Bear can answer Katie, Michael gives Katie a rub on the head.

"We're happy to be on this trip with you, too," says Michael. "Julia and I promised Uncle Charlie and Aunt Doris we'd make sure you don't get into any trouble, Katie."

Bear just shakes her head and woofs a soft bark.

"Now this is going to be fun to see!" continues Bear. "Katie not getting into *trouble*? It will be a first!"

Katie looks at Bear with a smirk on her face.

"Give me a break! I'm not always getting into trouble. Remember the time...?"

Bear, Michael and Julia all interrupt Katie at the same time with a friendly laugh.

"We love you Katie, old girl," says Julia, as she reaches for Bear's leash. "You are a very special dog and very mischievous too!"

"Let's take a walk while Uncle Charlie and Aunt Doris are checking out the souvenir shops. That will take quite some time, especially the way Aunt Doris shops," says Michael, looking at the big boats in the harbor. "I want to see some of the fishing boats."

"Well, I want to walk along the coast and see what has washed up on the shore," barks Katie, with her usual curious look.

"Oh, yes!" woofs Bear. "There are lots of
things to look for after high tide, you know. I just
love checking out the shoreline after high tide."

"I think Katie has a good idea. What do you
think, Julia?" asks Michael, excited. "I can
always see the boats when we get back."

"Okay," replies Julia. "Let's take Bear and
Katie along the shore to see what we can find."

Bear and Katie are happy that Michael and Julia want to walk along the shore, too.

"Oh, look what I found!" exclaims Julia. "It's a beach ball. Anyone for a game of fetch the ball?"

"Throw it to me, Julia, and I'll throw it to Katie. Then you get it from Katie then throw it to Bear," suggests Michael, as Julia picks up the beach ball.

The two Black Labs and the two kids are having lots of fun, throwing the ball back and forth to each other. Bear and Katie have big grins on their faces as they bark for the ball. They chase it down along the shoreline to retrieve it, carrying it back to Michael and Julia.

"Now this is a lot of fun!" barks Katie. "Throw it to me, and I'll retrieve it wherever it goes."

Julia picks up the beach ball and throws it a long way down the shore. Off Katie runs as fast as she can, showing off her Black Lab skills.

Suddenly, Katie takes a nosedive into the sand. She stops just short of an old boat, half in the sand and half in the marsh. Julia runs to see if Katie is okay, with Bear and Michael trailing right behind her.

"Are you all right, Katie girl?" asks Michael.

"Are you okay?" asks Julia.

"Wow! Are you okay?" barks Bear, all nervous. "That was one quick stop, with a nosedive, too, I might add."

"I'm alright, but that was a close call," whines Katie, as she looks at Michael with a sad look on her face, shaking the sand off her pretty black coat.

Michael reaches over and rubs sand off Katie's nose.

"Well, we're glad you're okay. We don't want anything to happen to our precious Katie."

Katie just smiles, cocking her head sideways and allowing Michael to give her one more rub on the nose.

Bear has already forgotten about Katie's near accident as she begins to look at the old boat, half buried in the sand.

"Hey! Come look at this!" barks Bear. "This boat is old. I mean *really* old!"

"You're right about that!" shouts Michael, running to take a closer look. "This is really old. I bet it's two hundred years old or even more."

"You really think so?" Julia whispers, as she looks up and down the old boat.

Katie jumps in. "Did I fall onto something, like a mystery? Did I discover something important?" she whispers.

"I think you might have," says Michael, as he begins to dig through the boat.

"Come on, Bear and Katie. I need your help clearing away the sand. You too, Julia," continues Michael.

The four begin to dig the sand out of the boat. Bear and Katie are tossing sand everywhere, their paws gently clutching at the wet sand and seaweed.

"Just imagine we are searching for a bone," laughs Bear.

"I can do that!" chuckles Katie as she digs with both paws, flinging sand in every direction. "But I hope we find something more exciting than a bone!"

All of a sudden, Michael looks up. He glances up and down the shoreline, making sure no one is looking their way. Then he gathers Julia, Bear and Katie around him.

"I think I found something!" whispers Michael, leaning in close.

With his hand he wipes sand off a metal box. "Look at this old box I found! I bet something important is in it!" He exclaims, clutching it close to his chest.

"You mean, like gold or something!" whispers Julia, excited and all covered in sand.

"Open it!" cries Bear with a very soft bark.

"Hurry!" cries Katie with a softer bark.

Michael hesitates for a moment. "Maybe we shouldn't open it. It might have something bad in it."

But Bear and Katie are too excited to wait.

"Oh come on!" says Bear. "What could be bad in a small metal box?"

Katie sits at attention. "Let's open it up, or we will never know. Right everybody?" she barks, wagging her tail and shivering all over. "I'm curious!"

"You're always curious, Katie. But this time, I have to agree with you," barks Bear.

"Okay!" replies Michael, a little bit uncertain but very, very curious. "I'll do it!"

Michael slowly opens the metal box. With extreme care he looks over its contents. "There's a map in it! Hmm! I wonder what for."

"Do you think it's a treasure map?" asks Julia jumping to her feet. "Maybe Bear and Katie can help us with the map."

"I don't know if it'll lead us to a treasure but I sure want to find out where it *will* lead us," Michael says eagerly, turning to Bear and Katie. "What do you two Labs think?"

Bear and Katie jump up and down, throwing themselves all over Michael. "Ruff, ruff," say the two dogs. "Count us in! We can sniff our way anywhere you want to go."

Michael steps aside and unfolds the map, straightening it from corner to corner. Then he carefully lays it on the ground. "Well now, let me take a few minutes to review this map. It's a bit old and wrinkled," he says.

After studying the map, he looks around. "According to this map, it looks like we need to go three hundred yards to the north. There we will see a small formation of rocks in the shape of a diamond," Michael continues.

Bear and Katie start to sniff, one Lab ahead of the other. Michael walks along with Katie, and Julia walks with Bear. Bear and Katie are taking this adventure very seriously.

Bear stops for a moment. "Well, I'd say we've gone three hundred yards but I don't see anything yet."

"Look around that bit of brush," suggests Katie. "Maybe the rocks are hidden, just like the boat was. It's probably been over two hundred years since the map was drawn."

"Good thinking, Katie!" agrees Michael. "Let's move some of this brush away, and look around."

"Over here!" shouts Julia. Bear sits at attention. "I think we found the small rock formation."

Michael and Katie run to the spot where Bear is sitting. "Yes! That's it. I'm sure it is! Just like the map shows," explains Michael, excited. "We just found our first clue!"

Bear is proud of herself. She stands up, points her nose up to the sky and takes a big whiff of salt air. "Now, what's next on the map?" barks Bear, impatiently.

"Well," says Michael, "we need to turn west and go another three hundred yards."

"But if we do that, it takes us away from the shoreline. I thought all treasures are hidden along the shore," says Julia, disappointment in her voice.

"Not always," says Michael. Sometimes, pirates buried their treasures away from the shore, because, just like you, they knew people would think the treasures will be near the shore."

"I know Bear and Katie will make sure we won't get lost. Right, girls?" says Julia, giving her two Lab friends a stern look.

"Right!" bark Bear and Katie at the same time. Bear looks at Julia with confidence, shaking her tail. "You'll never get lost with us around. Maybe into trouble, but not lost."

Bear walks past Julia and over to Katie. "Just kidding, Katie," says Bear as she giggles out a small bark.

"Oh, thanks!" grumps Katie, giving Bear a bulls-eye look. "You and Michael will be just fine as long as you are with us," she says.

Michael stops for a moment, thinking about stories he's heard about the small town of Searsport.

"You know Julia, Bear and Katie, this little town was once very important to merchants. Sea captains even settled here and some of their homes have secret passageways that lead out to the sea."

"Wow! That is so exciting," says Julia. "This is a special place."

"And, may I add," says Katie, "it has a very special boat buried with a great mystery!"

"Yes, Katie ol' girl, and we are going to find it!" yells Michael. "So, let's get going!"

Bear and Katie set off sniffing the ground, leading Michael and Julia toward the west to the next clue. Bear stops, and starts circling around and around. "Here we are," she says. "We have gone three hundred yards to the west. What does the map say next?"

Michael takes a good look at the map. "There should be a tree stump nearby which has a clue in it."

"Here it is!" cries Julia, "But it's been knocked over on its side."

"That's okay," replies Michael, "see if you can look inside of it."

Julia looks frantically. "Michael! I see a small jar hidden inside the tree stump, and there's something inside the jar!"

"Good! I bet that's the next clue," says Michael, rushing over. With his right hand he reaches in and removes it carefully.

"Well, what does it say?" barks Bear, wagging her tail in excitement.

"What does it say?" repeats Katie, wiggling all over.

"It says to 'follow the path that leads to out back, to a little shack,' " reads Michael.

"What ever could that mean?" says Julia, looking puzzled. "What does out back mean?"

"I remember hearing that many years ago, Maine was settled along the coast. Any land outside of the small towns and away from the coastline was referred to as 'Out Back'. People who built homes there called it 'Out Back.' Haven't you ever heard the expression 'Out Back Maine?' " Michael asks Julia.

"Oh, so that's what that means. I didn't know that."

"Well, then let's head "Out Back!" bark Bear and Katie, eager to continue their search.

"Okay! We're looking for a path that leads to a small shack," says Michael.

"I think I found it!" barks Bear. "Here's an old path. Now Katie and I will sniff until we find the shack."

Bear and Katie lead the way, sniffing carefully. The path is long, with tall weeds on both sides. "This path is part of the marsh, I believe," says Julia.

"Yep, you sure are right," says Michael. "Now we need to go a bit farther on the path and look for a small shack."

They continue on. Bear, in the lead, suddenly stops.

"How about a shed?" she barks. "I found a shed. Or ... is it a shack?"

"It looks more like a shed to me," says Katie, a bit uncertain.

The shack is hidden by large bushes, making it hard for Bear and Katie to know if it is a shed or a shack.

"The door looks as if it will be easy to get open," says Bear, "but I wonder about the corner of the door, I think it's jammed. That might give us some trouble."

"Michael pushes his way past Julia and the two Labs. "This must be it. "I'm going to try to get the door open and go inside."

"Are you sure you should do that?" cries Julia, who's very nervous.

"It's okay, Julia. I'll bet no one has been here for years. It's just an old shack," says Michael.

"I'll stay out here with Katie, if you don't mind!" exclaims Julia. "You and Bear can go inside."

Michael and Bear pull on the door, slightly opening it. "It's almost falling off its hinges," says Michael, as he bends down to peek through the cracks.

"Watch out, Bear. You'll have to step aside so I can get this door open a little farther. I don't want to get your nose caught in the door," says Michael.

"I don't want to get my nose caught in the door, either," replies Bear, moving out of the way.

"Now one more pull..." says Michael, his hands clutched tightly on the side of the door, grunting with every pull. "I believe I've got it now! Yes! I got it open!"

Bear, eager to get inside, squeezes her way past Michael. "I'm in!" woofs Bear. "Come on in, Michael. It's safe."

Michael follows Bear through the door. Julia and Katie stand outside, keeping guard.

"Well now, what do we have here?" wonders Michael.

"All I see is a bunch of paper and broken down furniture," whines Bear.

"Let's think like a pirate," suggests Michael. "Now, where would you hide secret papers?" Michael places his hand on his chin, rubbing it, deep in thought.

"If it were me, I would bury it, of course, because I'm a dog," says Bear. "But a person would hide it under a bed mattress! Or behind a picture! Or even behind a strip of wood in the room! Wouldn't he?" Bear continues, all excited.

"You're right, Bear. I'll look behind the strip of wood along the bottom of the wall first. Grab that sharp piece of wood, so I can pry this up," Michael says anxiously, kneeling down. "I just know the treasure must be here!"

"I can see something behind the wall!" says Bear as Michael loosens the woodwork.

"Here it is, Bear. I got it!" says Michael, jumping to his feet. "I have the treasure right here in this metal box! It looks just like the other box, where we found the map!"

Bear lets out three loud barks to signal to Katie and Julia that they found what they've been looking for. "The treasure!"

"Hurry! Hurry! Open it," cries Bear. Michael can hear Julia and Katie outside yelling for him to open the box.

"Okay, okay! I'll do it. Just give me a few seconds," he begs. "I need to catch my breath. I'm a bit nervous."

Michael and Bear bring the box outside and join Julia and Katie.

Bear and Katie sit down and anxiously wait for Michael to catch his breath. Julia just rolls her eyes and grins. "Okay, you've had your few seconds," barks Bear, so excited she can hardly sit still.

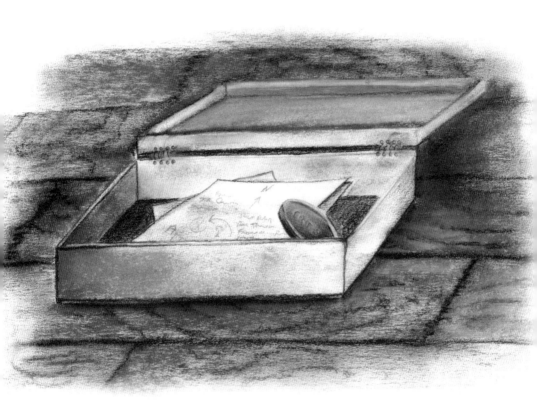

"All right, here I go!" says Michael, his hands shaking as he opens the metal box.

"It's another map! And one gold coin!" shouts Michael, all excited. "Do you realize what this means? All the searching we've done, and now we are closer to really finding that treasure!"

"What does the map say?" asks Julia. "Is there another clue?"

"Yes!" says Michael, glancing down at a small note attached to the map. "Oh, boy! It says to look at the inscription on the coin."

Julia takes the coin from Michael, grips it with her thumb and finger and takes a close look at it.

"All it says is TREASURE," answers Julia. "The coin just says TREASURE!"

"The note also says, 'There are many more hidden in the lighthouse,' " continues Michael.

"What lighthouse?" barks Bear. "Do you know how many lighthouses there are in Maine? I'll bet there are thirty or more."

"I think the lighthouse must be close by," says Julia. "The boat, map, clues and coin were all close by. So the lighthouse must be, too!"

"Well," says Katie, "There are four lighthouses in this area."

"But who is going to take us to the four lighthouses?" woofs Bear. "Our trip is over tomorrow. We'll be going back to New Hampshire."

"We'll need to have a talk with Uncle Charlie and Aunt Doris when they finish with their shopping, about our next trip to Maine," says Michael with a mischievous grin. "In the meantime, let's get back to the shore, so I can see the boats. I'll hold on to these maps and gold coin," he adds.

"Sounds good to us," bark the two black dogs. "Let's go!"

Michael, Julia, Bear and Katie all take off running as fast as they can to the shore.

Michael and Julia go look at the boats, while Bear and Katie sit close by to rest and wait for Mom and Dad to show up.

A few minutes later, Mom and Dad appear. Bear and Katie run to meet them. Michael and Julia aren't far behind.

"Well, how did you spend your day, girls?" Dad asks, as he pets his two favorite pooches on the head.

"We found a beach ball and played retrieve the ball," answers Bear.

"Yeah! That's what we did!" barks Katie, with a scheming look on her face. "Oh! By the way," she continues, "When will we be back this way? I want to look at some lighthouses."

"Lighthouses?" exclaims Dad. "I didn't now you and Bear were interested in lighthouses."

"Are you kidding? We love lighthouses," answer Bear and Katie, with three loud barks.

Michael and Julia laugh, and at the same time, both of them shout, "Bear and Katie love lighthouses, Uncle Charlie!"

The two enthusiastic Labs amuse Mom and Dad.

"Well, we are glad you love lighthouses, because it just so happens that we're coming back to Maine next weekend, to tour some lighthouses!" says Dad.

"And since you girls love lighthouses, we'll just bring you along," Mom tells them. "Perhaps Michael and Julia might enjoy tagging along, too? Since you all seem to have so much fun together," she continues.

Bear and Katie leap in the air with joy! They jump right on top of Michael and Julia, almost knocking them to the ground.

"Next weekend will be a big adventure for us," woofs Katie. And Bear agrees with a loud "Ruff! Ruff!"

Michael and Julia are so happy they take off running along the shore. Julia grabs the beach ball they were playing with earlier and throws it to Katie. Katie runs and jumps in the air. Bear rolls over and over, clapping her paws together. The four of them will find their treasure in the lighthouse after all!

Part Two

Bear and Katie
Love Lighthouses

It's only been a week since Bear and Katie spent a terrific weekend in Maine. They can't forget their trip to the little town of Searsport, where they found a mystery map that took them on a wild goose chase around the little town. Mom and Dad are anxious to return to Maine this weekend to visit some lighthouses, and so are the two Black Labs.

Bear and Katie have suggested they go to Camden and Rockport, two towns near Searsport, so they can continue following the mystery map in their quest for the treasure. They are convinced that the treasure is hidden in one of the lighthouses nearby. Mom and Dad have no idea why Bear and Katie picked those particular places to go, but they know their instincts are good and they want to oblige the two Black Labs.

"Bear, this is going to be interesting! Don't you think so?" asks Katie with a whisper as she wiggles her way into a comfortable spot in the truck.

"Sh...!" says Bear. "We don't want Mom and Dad to hear us, they might change their minds."

"We don't want that to happen! I want to find that treasure once and for all," woofs Katie.

"I sure am glad you remembered to ask Dad to pick up Michael and Julia," says Katie with a yip. "That was good thinking on your part, Bear."

Bear gives Katie a big grin, trying not to look too proud. "We're just lucky that Mom and Dad enjoy taking their niece, nephew and pets with them when they travel," she says.

"Right!" Katie agrees. "And we need them! Michael sure reads maps well."

An hour drive brings them to Portland, where Michael and Julia are waiting impatiently to see their friends Bear and Katie.

"Look, Katie! There's Michael and Julia," says Bear with excitement.

"Hi! Bear and Katie!" Michael and Julia wave as they come running to join the Labs.

Michael and Julia head around the truck and clamber up into the back seat. Julia reaches over and gives Bear and Katie a big hug around the neck.

Bear, Katie, Michael, Julia, Mom and Dad all make their way up the seacoast to the small town of Camden.

Camden is one of Maine's most charming seaports, a beautiful place *"where the mountains meet the sea,"* as the locals all say. From the lookout point above the town, you can gaze down on all of Camden and its lovely harbor. "No wonder Dad is anxious to get his camera out to do some photography," thinks Bear.

"Let's run over to the picnic table and see what Mom is reading," barks Bear.

Katie takes off, leading the way. Bear, Michael and Julia are not far behind her, when Katie reaches the table.

"Now, let's see," says Mom, taking a look at her brochures. "Along the coast here, there are several lighthouses. We have Owls Head Light, Grindel Point, Curtis Light, and to the north, we have Fort Point Light," she tells them.

"Which one is closest to Searsport?" asks Bear.

"I believe it's the Fort Point Light," answers Mom. "But I don't think we will get to that one today."

Bear looks at Katie, and then to Michael and Julia with an expression of disappointment on her face. "I believe the treasure must be hidden in the Fort Point Light," she whispers to them. Katie agrees and both are convinced the treasure is hidden there.

"That's okay," Michael whispers back to them. "Yes, it's a good thing," murmurs Julia. "If we tour the other three lighthouses today, we'll be able to spend more time at Fort Point tomorrow. We will need a lot of time to search for the treasure."

"Julia's right," agrees Katie.

Bear and Katie turn to Mom and Dad and give them a loud bark. "Let's go see some lighthouses!" shout the two Black Labs.

"Let's go see some lighthouses!" shout Michael and Julia, almost as loud.

The first lighthouse they visit is Owls Head. Mom gets out her brochure and reads. "A short knob-like light overlooks the south side entrance to Rockland Harbor. After it was built in 1825, it quickly deteriorated. The last keeper complained when he wrote, 'It is in a state of extreme dilapidation and decay, from top to bottom.' The lighthouse was repaired and today it shines 100 feet above Penobscot Bay, in the Rockland Harbor."

"Wow!" woofs Bear. "I sure am glad they repaired it. It's just beautiful. Look at all the steps up to it!"

Katie is amazed. "I never knew there was so much history to them. Isn't the harbor just lovely?"

Michael bends down and gives Bear a big bear hug, and Julia pets Katie on the head. They are proud of their favorite Black Labs. The two children love spending time with the two smartest dogs in the world.

Michael nudges Julia. "Lets take a walk with Bear and Katie, so we can get closer to it," Michael suggests.

"Good idea!" says Julia. "Come on Bear and Katie, we're going for a little walk."

The two dogs look at each other and with a soft woof, they take off.

"Do you think the treasure is here, Michael?" asks Bear.

"I don't know. What do you think?" he asks.

"I don't think it's here," says Bear with a shake of her head. "My instincts tell me it's waiting for us at the Fort Point Light."

"You're probably right," says Michael. "But in order to search Fort Point, we have to convince Uncle Charlie and Aunt Doris that we all want to take our time touring all the lighthouses. Then it won't seem strange when we take our time at Fort Point."

"All I have to say is I enjoy the history," barks Katie. "I'm learning all sorts of things."

"You got that right!" says Bear, jumping in. "I'm finding this to be very educational and lots of fun, I might add."

With a wave of his hand, Uncle Charlie motions for the children and the two Labs. "Time for the next lighthouse," he calls.

The next stop is the Curtis Light. "Curtis Light protects the entrance of Camden Harbor," Mom reads. "The island it sits on was called Negro Island, for a black cook accompanying Captain John Smith during his visit here, back in the 17th Century. The island was renamed Curtis Island in 1934, after a publisher and town patron named Cyrus HK Curtis. The light now belongs to the town of Camden."

"They must have really liked that cook's cooking," barks Bear, "for a light to be named after him. They must have thought a lot of him."

"How about a light called Bear and Katie?" chuckles Katie.

Michael and Julia laugh. "Katie, you are so funny!" giggles Julia, giving Katie a pat on the head.

"Let's take another walk," says Michael.

"What a beautiful lighthouse!" exclaims Julia. "It's such a beautiful day. The sky is perfect, the sun is shining and it's so nice and warm." Bear and Katie give Julia a paws-up. They are enjoying this trip as much as the children.

"How about we take a lunch break?" suggests Dad. "Then we can head up the coast to Lincolnville. That's where we catch the ferry over to the island of Islesboro. There's a nice lighthouse I think you Labs and kids would really enjoy seeing."

"A ride on a ferry?" says Bear, excited.

"Oh boy!" jumps Katie. "I've never been on a ferry before."

"I can't wait!" agrees Michael.

"I've never been on a ferry either, Katie," shouts Julia, jumping up and down while holding Katie's leash. "This is going to be so cool!"

The family has lunch, and then follows the winding coast to the small town of Lincolnville. They arrive just in time to meet the boat. There are several cars waiting to drive aboard the small ferry to Islesboro. "This is your lucky day! There's room for one more," shouts the ferryman. "Come on aboard!"

After parking the truck, the whole family gets out to enjoy the fresh sea air. The day is magnificent. The hot sun beams down on their faces.

Katie runs around and around the boat. She is so excited, she doesn't want to miss out on one bit of scenery.

Just as she rounds a corner, she slips, loses her balance and goes flying overboard!

Julia sees Katie fall in the water. "Hurry!"
she shouts. "Katie's fallen overboard!"

Everyone on the boat runs to see what all the
commotion is about. Katie, paddling as hard
and as fast as she can barks, "Wait for me!"

Everyone begins to cheer her on. Katie is
proud of her swimming skills, and decides to
show off. She does a little circle around and
around, followed by a dive.

Bear, worried about Katie, isn't at all amused. "This isn't a lake, you know!" she calls to her friend. "This is the ocean! You better hurry and get back on this boat or some big old shark is going to have you for lunch!"

Katie stops her fooling around and quickly swims back to the boat. She doesn't want to be anyone's lunch. Dad is there to help her on board. Katie soaks everyone as she gives herself three good shakes, flinging water in every direction.

"You really scared me, Katie," whimpers Bear.

"I'm sorry, Bear. I didn't mean to fall off the boat. It just happened," says Katie with a look of guilt on her face. "I won't run around the boat anymore. I promise."

"Well, we are pulling into the shore now anyway," says Michael, who is still a little nervous over Katie's unscheduled swim. "I'll be glad to get off and go see the lighthouse."

The family drives off the ferry and over to the other side of the island. Long before they arrive, they can see their third lighthouse for the day, the beautiful Grindel Point Light. "It's square!" exclaims Julia. "Read to us about it, Aunt Doris."

"The Grindel Point Light sits at the entrance of Gilkey Harbor," reads Mom. "It stands thirty-three feet high, and it was built in 1853."

"I think we should check out this lighthouse really well," whispers Michael, "since it's on an island."

"Good thinking," says Julia. "If I were a pirate, I'd hide my treasure on an island."

Bear stops and sits for a moment. "I still
have a feeling we're going to find the treasure
at the Fort Point Lighthouse," she says. "I
don't know why, I just feel it in my bones."

"I have to agree with Bear," says Katie.
"Bear's smart, she knows everything!"

"Well, thank you, Katie! That's the nicest
thing you ever said about me," grins Bear. Katie
just wags her tail and cuddles up next to her
best friend.

"Okay!" says Michael, "Let's just take a nice long walk around the island and enjoy the rest of the day. Tonight we'll all get together and discuss our plans for tomorrow."

The two kids and two Labs tour the lighthouse and enjoy Islesboro. Dad and Mom take time out to get everyone ice cream at a small store on the island while they wait for the ferry to take them back to the mainland.

"I hope you don't fall off the boat again," growls Bear, giving Katie one of her 'don't even think about it,' looks.

"I won't," chuckles Katie "I don't want to meet with any big fish today."

The ride back to the mainland is pleasant, and Katie behaves herself. As soon as the ferry docks back in Lincolnville, Dad heads up the coast to their cottage, where they will be spending the night. Tomorrow will be a big day for everyone.

After dinner, Michael and Julia take Bear and Katie for a walk along the shore, making their plans to find the treasure.

Bear lies down and looks at Michael. "Do you have the mystery map with you?" she asks.

"I have it right here in my pocket," replies Michael. He pulls out the map and unfolds it carefully.

"Okay, let's examine it--and the gold coin," says Bear anxiously.

"You do have the gold coin, don't you?" asks Katie.

"I gave it to Julia to hold," says Michael.

"Don't worry, I have it right here," Julia jumps in. "I want to find more just like it!" She pulls out the beautiful golden coin with the mysterious word "TREASURE" written on it.

"I figure that the treasure is probably in the base of the lighthouse, or hidden near the light," whispers Michael. "Two of us can search the base and two can search up in the tower around the light."

"Katie and I will search the base of the lighthouse if you don't mind," says Julia, carefully putting the coin back in her pocket. "You know me. I'm scared of heights."

"Okay! Then Bear and I will go up and check out the light," says Michael. "We need to get to bed early so we can get an early start." Refolding the map he adds, "It might take us half the day to find it."

"You're right," says Bear. "We really need to go back to the cottage and settle in for the night."

"I'll beat you all to the cottage!" yells Katie, and off they all run.

The following day, Dad and Mom, the kids and the two Black Labs are anxious about visiting the Fort Point Light. But first they must stop in Belfast, a town only ten miles from Searsport.

Bear and Katie are hungry. Michael and Julia are sure they need a lot of energy for the big treasure hunt. They enjoy breakfast on the deck of a lovely restaurant overlooking Penobscot Bay.

After breakfast and a short walk, Bear, Katie, Michael and Julia are excited as they climb into the truck and take their seats. They know they are very close to where the treasure is hidden. It's only a few miles out of town.

On the way to the lighthouse Dad spots a sign. "Pirates Museum! Humm!" he says rubbing his chin.

Bear, Katie, Michael and Julia look at each other, all excited.

Bear barks three times, "Pirates Museum! Did you say Pirates Museum? Stop!" She says, "I . . . mean, can we stop?" Bear continues, quietly, trying to cover up her sudden burst of excitement.

Dad stops at the museum in Searsport. There Bear and Katie, Michael and Julia gather all sorts of information about pirates.

"The more we learn about pirates, the more we will be able to figure out where the pirates hid the treasure." Says Michael.

Bear and Katie sniff around the museum for any clues that can help them, while Michael and Julia listen to the tour guide's every word.

How far is the Fort Point Light from here?"
Mom asks the tour guide.

"Just a few miles north of here," he tells her.
"Just as you pass Stockton Springs, you make a
right turn and that will take you right to the
lighthouse. You can't miss it." He continues.

"Well then!" Says Dad all excited. "Let's go
see another lighthouse."

Bear and Katie run out of the museum,
pulling Michael and Julia behind them, as they
hold on tight to their leashes. Mom and Dad
chuckle at the two excited Labs.

With only a few miles to go, Bear and Katie
watch out the window with anticipation.

"Oh look! I see the lighthouse! I can't wait to get out and start searching," says Bear with her nose wiggling.

Me too!" barks Katie. "I see the lighthouse."

"Oh boy! Uncle Charlie is stopping the truck," says Michael.

Dad can hardly open the truck door before Bear and Katie shoot out like bullets. Michael and Julia are already out of the truck.

"Well! I guess you four do like lighthouses," laughs Dad. "I understand the kids liking them, but I never expected two Black Labs to take such an interest in lighthouses. Let's go see what this one is all about."

Mom gets out her brochure one more time. "The Fort Point Light was built at the entrance of Cape Jellison," she reads. "It sits on the original sight of Fort Pownall, which was built by the British in 1759, to keep the French military out of the bay. The lighthouse was built in 1836 to guide ships into the upper Penobscot Bay. It deteriorated within a few years, but was rebuilt in 1857. The Fort Point light's white bell tower, 250 feet northeast of the lighthouse, still holds the giant fog bell, built in Boston, that served as a fog signal until 1960."

"Now this light really has a lot of history," woofs Bear.

"It sure does! I can imagine how it must have been," says Katie.

"Okay, let's get going, and look this place over good," whispers Julia.

"Uncle Charlie and Aunt Doris are off taking pictures," says Michael. "This is our chance to find our treasure. Julia and Katie, you search around the base. You come with me Bear, we'll go this way."

Julia and Katie are looking frantically for the treasure. Around and around the square base they go. Katie is sniffing every piece of ground, as she searches for the treasure.

Bear and Michael hurry inside and start up the tower. "I don't get it," says Michael. "It's round inside--even though it's square outside!"

"Yes," replies Bear. "This is the second lighthouse we've visited that is square on the outside."

As soon as Bear reaches the top, she starts sniffing around by the light, her nose to the floor. Both labs are putting their keen sense of smell to good use today. Suddenly, Bear sits and barks three barks, her signal for Katie to come and join her.

Katie quickly appears at the top of the stairs. "What is it, Bear?" she asks, anticipation in her voice.

"Katie, I think I'm on to something!" whines Bear, shaking with excitement. "What do you think?"

Katie puts her nose down, then up, then down again. "Smells like coins to me!" barks Katie. "I think we may have sniffed out the old treasure! Whoopee!"

Michael and Julia run to join Bear and Katie. "Let me take a look," says Michael, looking through a crack in the frame that holds the big light. "I see something! I...really see something!" he shouts.

"Reach your hand in and grab it!" cries Bear, almost speechless.

"Get it!" cries Katie.

"Go on, Michael," whispers Julia, "It must be the treasure!"

Michael is so nervous his hand shakes as he reaches through the small opening. "I've got something!" he shouts with joy. "I've got something! The treasure sure is here because here's another coin! And there's a letter with it."

"What does it say?" woofs Bear, trembling all over.

"It says, 'collect the coins and read them.' Now what can that mean?" he wonders. "Hurry! Give me that coin, Julia."

Julia takes the coin out of her pocket and passes it over to Michael. Bear and Katie dig frantically for the others through the opening of the door. "Let's lay them on the floor next to each other and read what they say," suggests Bear.

Michael lays the coins one at a time on the floor. Each coin has a word written on it. The words 'FIND' and 'LYING' and 'GUARD' and 'DELIGHT' appear. And then 'NIGHT' and 'SEA' and 'WATCH' and 'DAY.' Michael lays their first coin down with the rest, the shiny coin that says, 'TREASURE.' All in all, there are twenty-eight coins.

"What does the message say?" ask Bear and Katie. "Read it for us!"

"First we have to put this in some kind of order," says Julia, puzzling over the words. "I see some words that rhyme." She picks up the coins that say 'HERE' and 'NEAR.' Michael picks up the coins that say 'DELIGHT' and 'NIGHT.'

Julia makes a rhyme out of her two coins. "AS I WATCH THE GREAT SEA HERE, HE FINDS MY COINS AND TREASURE NEAR."

"That doesn't make sense," says Michael shaking his head. He tries a rhyme with his two coins. "MY TREASURE HERE FINDS NEAR DELIGHT, SEA LYING COINS WHO WATCH THE NIGHT."

"That's as crazy as my rhyme," frets Julia. Michael moves some coins around and Julia moves a few more. Again and again, they try changing the order.

"We'll never figure this out!" cries Michael.

"Wait a second!" whispers Julia. "How about this?" She moves three coins then steps back to look at the rhyme in front of them.

"HE WHO FINDS THE TREASURE HERE, KNOW THAT I AM LYING NEAR. I GUARD MY COINS, BOTH DAY AND NIGHT, AS I WATCH THE SEA WITH GREAT DELIGHT."

"That's it!" exclaims Michael.

"Oh, that is so sad," cries Julia.

"It sure is," whines Bear.

"I feel bad for him," whimpers Katie, hanging her head.

Michael, Julia, Bear and Katie all look at each other. For a moment they are silent, thinking about the message of the coins."

"I don't think we should disturb them," says Michael. "What would happen to the pirate, if we took his coins?"

"He wouldn't have anything to guard anymore," answers Bear.

"I vote that we leave the treasure where it is, with the pirate," suggests Bear.

"Me too!" shouts Katie. "It belongs to the pirate anyway!"

"You know what is really important is that we found the treasure," says Julia, "and we had a lot of fun doing it, too."

"We learned a lot, too," adds Katie. "I really enjoyed hearing about lighthouses, and I got to go swimming in the ocean," she chuckles.

"And we've discovered that the four of us make one good team," adds Bear.

"I sure had fun, and I hope we get to go on another adventure together soon," says Michael with a big smile.

"Me too," cries Julia, hugging Katie.

So Michael, Julia, Bear and Katie, all agree to leave the treasure with the pirate. Michael and Bear climb the stairs to the tower and place the coins back where they found them.

"Now the pirate can continue to look out at the sea that he loves so much," barks Bear, and she and Michael return from the tower.

Katie runs out of the lighthouse and over toward the small pyramid-shaped building that houses the fog bell. Barking happily, she races back to the lighthouse with Bear right at her heels. Then Michael and Julia join in. They all run around the lighthouse, chasing each other and laughing joyfully.

Mom and Dad, watching them from a distance, just shake their heads and laugh, too.

"What wonderful children!" says Mom.

"What wonderful dogs," says Dad. "It's nice they enjoy visiting lighthouses so much." They look at each other and with a smile they say, "Bear and Katie sure love lighthouses!"

The End

About Bear

Bear is gentle, caring, very intelligent and quick thinking. She always obeys the rules and loves playing the role of Katie's protector. Her hobbies include riding around with Dad, retrieving balls and chasing squirrels. Bear welcomes a pat on the head from everyone she meets. Bear, a female black lab/shepherd mix, wandered her way to our doorstep when she was only six weeks old. Bear always wears a collar.

About Katie

Katie is fun loving, a bit too friendly, and is always getting into trouble. She loves her best friend Bear and knows Bear will always come to her rescue. Katie finds trouble everywhere she goes. Her hobbies are swimming, retrieving balls and frisbee. She was rescued at the last minute from a dog pound when she was six months old. Katie is a female black lab. Katie prefers to wear a scarf.

About the Author

Loni R. Burchette was born in
Ashland, Kentucky. It was
only when she moved to New
Hampshire that she finally
found a place she could love as much as the
beautiful "Blue Grass State" she hails from.
Along with her husband and four of her five
children, she now makes the Lakes Region of
New Hampshire her home. Her hobbies are
writing, art and traveling.

About the Illustrator

Patricia Sweet-MacDonald was
born in Clearwater, Florida.
She moved to New Hampshire
in 2002, with her husband,
Michael and two children, Alison and Brendan.
She started painting at age 5 and has never quit.

Future Bear and Katie Books

A Day With Friends

A Riverboat Ride on the Ohio

Bear and Katie's "Christmas in New England"

A Day at the Beach and Katie gets arrested

Bear and Katie at the Kentucky Derby
     "Run for the Roses"

Lost in the White Mountains

Bear and Katie go to Ireland "Kiss of the
     Blarney stone"

In the Badlands with Mr. Wanbli (Eagle)

A Day with Mato the Bear

Visit our website at www.bearandkatie.com